KT-363-630

To Sophie
R.D.

The
ENORMOUS CROCODILE

PUFFIN BOOKS

Published by the Penguin Group
Penguin Books Ltd, 80 Strand, London WC2R 0RL, England
Penguin Group (USA) Inc., 375 Hudson Street, New York, New York 10014, USA
Penguin Group (Canada), 90 Eglinton Avenue East, Suite 700, Toronto, Ontario, Canada M4P 2Y3
(a division of Pearson Penguin Canada Inc.)
Penguin Ireland, 25 St Stephen's Green, Dublin 2, Ireland (a division of Penguin Books Ltd)
Penguin Group (Australia), 707 Collins Street, Melbourne, Victoria 3008, Australia
(a division of Pearson Australia Group Pty Ltd)
Penguin Books India Pvt Ltd, 11 Community Centre, Panchsheel Park, New Delhi – 110 017, India
Penguin Group (NZ), 67 Apollo Drive, Rosedale, Auckland 0632, New Zealand
(a division of Pearson New Zealand Ltd)
Penguin Books (South Africa) (Pty) Ltd, Block D, Rosebank Office Park,
181 Jan Smuts Avenue, Parktown North, Gauteng 2193, South Africa

Penguin Books Ltd, Registered Offices: 80 Strand, London WC2R 0RL, England

www.puffinbooks.com

First published by Jonathan Cape Ltd 1978
Published by Puffin Books 1980
This edition published 2013
006

Text copyright © Roald Dahl Nominee Ltd, 1978
Illustrations copyright © Quentin Blake, 1978
All rights reserved

The moral right of the author and illustrator has been asserted

Set in Goudy Old Style

Printed in China

Except in the United States of America, this book is sold subject
to the condition that it shall not, by way of trade or otherwise, be lent,
re-sold, hired out, or otherwise circulated without the publisher's
prior consent in any form of binding or cover other than that in
which it is published and without a similar condition including this
condition being imposed on the subsequent purchaser

British Library Cataloguing in Publication Data
A CIP catalogue record for this book is available from the British Library

ISBN: 978-0-141-34647-2

www.greenpenguin.co.uk

MIX
Paper from
responsible sources
FSC
www.fsc.org   FSC® C018179

Penguin Books is committed to a sustainable
future for our business, our readers and our planet.
This book is made from Forest Stewardship
Council™ certified paper.

ROALD DAHL

The ENORMOUS CROCODILE

ILLUSTRATED BY QUENTIN BLAKE

PUFFIN

In the biggest, brownest muddiest river in Africa, two crocodiles lay with their heads just above the water. One of the crocodiles was enormous. The other was not so big.

"Do you know what I would like for my lunch today?" the Enormous Crocodile asked.

"No," the Notsobig One said. "What?"

The Enormous Crocodile grinned, showing hundreds of sharp white teeth. "For my lunch today," he said, "I would like a nice juicy little child."

"I never eat children," the Notsobig One said. "Only fish."

"Ho, ho, ho!" cried the Enormous Crocodile. "I'll bet if you saw a fat juicy little child paddling in the water over there at this very moment, you'd gulp him up in one gollop!"

"No, I wouldn't," the Notsobig One said. "Children are too tough and chewy. They are tough and chewy and nasty and bitter."

"*Tough* and *chewy*!" cried the Enormous Crocodile. "*Nasty* and *bitter*! What awful tommy-rot you talk! They are juicy and yummy!"

"They taste so bitter," the Notsobig One said, "you have to cover them with sugar before you can eat them."

"Children are bigger than fish," said the Enormous Crocodile. "You get bigger helpings."

"You are greedy," the Notsobig One said. "You're the greediest croc in the whole river."

"I'm the bravest croc in the whole river," said the Enormous Crocodile. "I'm the only one who dares to leave the water and go through the jungle to the town to look for little children to eat."

"You've only done that once," snorted the Notsobig One. "And what happened then? They all saw you coming and ran away."

"Ah, but today when I go, they won't see me at all," said the Enormous Crocodile.

"Of course they'll see you," the Notsobig One said. "You're so enormous and ugly, they'll see you from miles away."

The Enormous Crocodile grinned again, and his terrible sharp teeth sparkled like knives in the sun. "Nobody will see me," he said, "because this time I've thought up secret plans and clever tricks."

"*Clever tricks?*" cried the Notsobig One. "You've never done anything clever in your life! You're the stupidest croc on the whole river!"

"I'm the cleverest croc on the whole river," the Enormous Crocodile answered. "For my lunch today I shall feast upon a fat juicy little child while you lie here in the river feeling hungry. Goodbye."

The Enormous Crocodile swam to the side of the river, and crawled out of the water.

A gigantic creature was standing in the slimy oozy mud on the river-bank. It was Humpy-Rumpy, the Hippopotamus.

"Hello, hello," said Humpy-Rumpy. "Where on earth are you off to at this time of day?"

"I have secret plans and clever tricks," said the Crocodile.

"Oh dear," said Humpy-Rumpy. "I'll bet you're going to do something horrid."

The Enormous Crocodile grinned at
Humpy-Rumpy and said:

> "*I'm going to fill my*
> *hungry empty tummy*
> *With something yummy*
> *yummy yummy yummy!*"

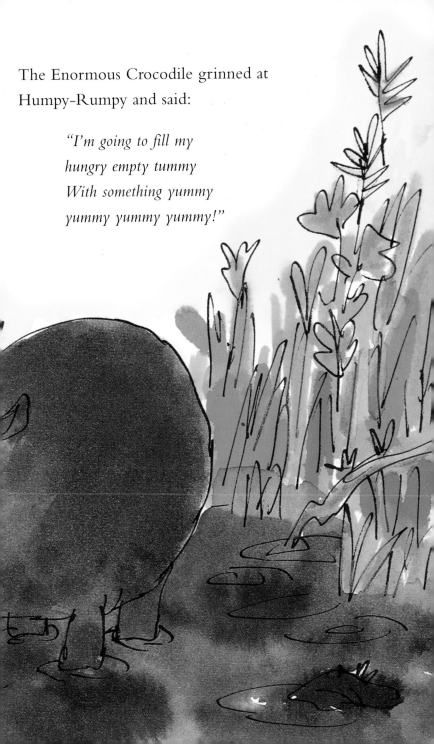

"What's so yummy?" asked Humpy-Rumpy.

"Try to guess," said the Crocodile. "It's something that walks on two legs."

"You don't mean . . ." said Humpy-Rumpy. "You don't *really* mean you're going to eat a little child?"

"Of course I am," said the Crocodile.

"Oh, you horrid greedy grumptious brute!" cried Humpy-Rumpy. "I hope you get caught and cooked and turned into crocodile soup!"

The Enormous Crocodile laughed out loud at Humpy-Rumpy. Then he waddled off into the jungle.

Inside the jungle, he met Trunky, the Elephant. Trunky was nibbling leaves from the top of a tall tree, and he didn't notice the Crocodile at first. So the Crocodile bit him on the leg.

"Ow!" said Trunky in his big deep voice. "Who did that? Oh, it's you, is it, you beastly Crocodile. Why don't you go back to the big brown muddy river where you belong?"

"I have secret plans and clever tricks," said
the Crocodile.

"You mean you've *nasty* plans and *nasty* tricks,"
said Trunky. "You've never done a nice thing in
your life."

The Enormous Crocodile grinned up at Trunky
and said:

> *"I'm off to find a yummy*
> *child for lunch.*
> *Keep listening and you'll hear*
> *the bones go crunch!"*

"Oh, you wicked beastly beast!" cried Trunky. "Oh, you foul and filthy fiend! I hope you get squashed and squished and squizzled and boiled up into crocodile stew!"

The Enormous Crocodile laughed out loud and disappeared into the thick jungle.

A bit further on, he met Muggle-Wump, the Monkey. Muggle-Wump was sitting in a tree, eating nuts.

"Hello, Crocky," said Muggle-Wump. "What are you up to now?"

"I have secret plans and clever tricks," said the Crocodile.

"Would you like some nuts?" asked Muggle-Wump.

"I have better things to eat than nuts," sniffed the Crocodile.

"I didn't think there *was* anything better than nuts," said Muggle-Wump.

"Ah-ha," said the Enormous Crocodile,

> *"The sort of things that*
> *I'm going to eat*
> *have fingers, toe-nails, arms*
> *and legs and feet!"*

Muggle-Wump went pale and began to shake all over. "You aren't really going to gobble up a little child, are you?" he said.

"Of course I am," said the Crocodile. "Clothes and all. They taste better with the clothes on."

"Oh, you horrid hoggish croc!" cried Muggle-Wump. "You slimy creature! I hope the buttons and buckles all stick in your throat and choke you to death!"

The Crocodile grinned up at Muggle-Wump and said, "I eat monkeys, too." And quick as a flash, with one bite of his huge jaws, he bit through the tree that Muggle-Wump was sitting in, and down it came.

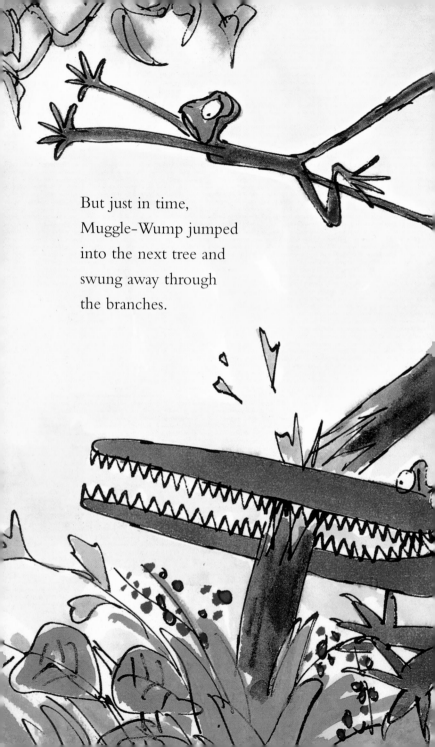

But just in time,
Muggle-Wump jumped
into the next tree and
swung away through
the branches.

A bit further on, the Enormous Crocodile met the Roly-Poly Bird. The Roly-Poly Bird was building a nest in an orange tree.

"Hello there, Enormous Crocodile!" sang the Roly-Poly Bird. "We don't often see you up here in the jungle."

"Ah," said the Crocodile. "I have secret plans and clever tricks."

"I hope it's not something nasty," sang the Roly-Poly Bird.

"*Nasty!*" cried the Crocodile. "Of course it's not nasty! It's delicious!"

"It's luscious, it's super,
It's mushious, it's duper,
It's better than rotten old fish.
You mash it and munch it,
You chew it and crunch it!
It's lovely to hear it go squish!"

"It must be berries," sang the Roly-Poly
Bird. "Berries are my favourite food in the
world. Is it raspberries, perhaps? Or could it
be strawberries?"

The Enormous Crocodile laughed so much his
teeth rattled together like pennies in a moneybox.
"Crocodiles don't eat berries," he said. "We eat little
boys and girls. And sometimes we eat Roly-Poly
Birds, as well." Very quickly, the Crocodile reached
up and snapped his jaws at the Roly-Poly Bird.
He just missed the Bird, but he managed to
catch hold of the long beautiful feathers in its
tail. The Roly-Poly Bird gave a shriek of
terror and shot straight up into the air,
leaving its tail feathers behind in the
Enormous Crocodile's mouth.

At last, the Enormous Crocodile came out of the
other side of the jungle into the sunshine. He could
see the town not far away.

"Ho-ho!" he said, talking aloud to himself.

"Ha-ha! That walk through the jungle has made me
hungrier than ever. One child isn't going to be
nearly enough for me today. I won't be full up until

I've eaten at least three juicy little children!"

He started to creep forward towards the town.

The Enormous Crocodile crept over to a place where there were a lot of coconut trees.

He knew that children from the town often came here looking for coconuts. The trees were too tall for them to climb, but there were always some coconuts on the ground that had fallen down.

The Enormous Crocodile quickly collected all the coconuts that were lying on the ground. He also gathered together several fallen branches.

"Now for Clever Trick Number One!" he whispered to himself. "It won't be long before I am eating the first part of my lunch!"

He took all the coconut branches and held them between his teeth.

He grasped the coconuts in his front paws. Then he stood straight up in the air, balancing himself on his tail.

He arranged the branches and the coconuts so cleverly that he now looked exactly like a small coconut tree standing among the big coconut trees.

Soon, two children came along. They were brother and sister. The boy was called Toto. His sister was called Mary. They walked around looking for fallen coconuts, but they couldn't find any because the Enormous Crocodile had gathered them all up.

"Oh look!" cried Toto. "That tree over there is much smaller than the others! And it's full of coconuts! I think I could climb that one quite easily if you help me up the first bit."

Toto and Mary ran towards what they thought was the small coconut tree.

The Enormous Crocodile peered through the branches, watching them as they came closer and closer. He licked his lips. He began to dribble with excitement.

Suddenly there was a tremendous whooshing noise. It was Humpy-Rumpy, the Hippopotamus. He came crashing and snorting out of the jungle. His head was down low and he was galloping at a terrific speed.

"Look out, Toto!" shouted Humpy-Rumpy. "Look out, Mary! That's not a coconut tree! It's the Enormous Crocodile and he wants to eat you up!"

Humpy-Rumpy charged straight at the Enormous Crocodile.

He caught him with his giant head and sent him tumbling and skidding over the ground.

"Ow-eeee!" cried the Crocodile. "Help! Stop! Where am I?"

Toto and Mary ran back to the town as fast as they could.

But crocodiles are tough. It is difficult for even a hippopotamus to hurt them.

The Enormous Crocodile picked himself up and crept towards the place where the children's playground was.

"Now for Clever Trick Number Two!" he said to himself. "This one is certain to work!"

There were no children in the playground at that moment. They were all in school.

The Enormous Crocodile found a large piece of wood and placed it in the middle of the playground. Then he lay across the piece of wood and tucked in his feet so that he looked almost exactly like a see-saw.

When school was over, the children all came running on to the playground.

"Oh look!" they cried. "We've got a new see-saw!"

They all crowded round, shouting with excitement.

"Bags I have the first go!"

"I'll get on the other end!"

"I want to go first!"

"So do I! So do I!"

Then, a girl who was older than the others said, "It's rather a funny knobbly sort of a see-saw, isn't it? Do you think it'll be safe to sit on?"

"Of course it will!" the others said. "It looks strong as anything!"

The Enormous Crocodile opened one eye just a tiny bit and watched the children who were crowding around him. Soon, he thought, one of them is going to sit on my head, then I will give a jerk and a snap, and after that it will be *yum yum yum*.

At that moment, there was a flash of brown and something jumped into the playground and hopped up on to the top of the swings.

It was Muggle-Wump, the Monkey.

"Run!" Muggle-Wump shouted to the children. "All of you, run, run, run! That's not a see-saw! It's the Enormous Crocodile and he wants to eat you up!"

The children screamed and ran for their lives.

Muggle-Wump disappeared back into the jungle, and the Enormous Crocodile was left all alone in the playground.

He cursed the Monkey and waddled back into the bushes to hide.

"I'm getting hungrier and hungrier!" he said. "I shall have to eat at least four children now before I am full up!"

The Enormous Crocodile crept around the edge of the town, taking great care not to be seen.

He came to a place where they were getting ready to have a fair. There were slides and swings and dodgem-cars and people selling popcorn and candy-floss. There was also a big roundabout.

The roundabout had marvellous wooden creatures for the children to ride on. There were white horses and lions and tigers and mermaids with fishes' tails and fearsome dragons with red tongues sticking out of their mouths.

"Now for Clever Trick Number Three," said the

Enormous Crocodile, licking his lips.

When no one was looking, he crept up on to the roundabout and put himself between a wooden lion and a fearsome dragon. He sat up a bit on his back legs and he kept very still. He looked exactly like a wooden crocodile on the roundabout.

Soon, all sorts of children came flocking into the fair. Several of them ran towards the roundabout. They were very excited.

"I'm going to ride on a dragon!" cried one.

"I'm going on a lovely white horse!"
cried another.

"I'm going on a lion!" cried a third one.

And one little girl, whose name was Jill said, "*I'm going to ride on that funny old wooden crocodile!*"

The Enormous Crocodile kept very still, but he could see the little girl coming towards him. "Yummy-yum-yum," he thought. "I'll gulp her up easily in one gollop."

Suddenly there was a *swish* and a *swoosh* and something came swishing and swooshing out of the sky.

It was the Roly-Poly Bird.

He flew round and round the roundabout, singing, "Look out, Jill! Look out. Look out. Don't ride on that crocodile!"

Jill stopped and looked up.

"That's not a wooden crocodile!" sang the Roly-Poly Bird. "It's a real one! It's the Enormous Crocodile from the river and he wants to eat you up!"

Jill turned and ran. So did all the other children. Even the man who was working the roundabout jumped off it and ran away as fast as he could.

The Enormous Crocodile cursed the Roly-Poly Bird and waddled back into the bushes to hide.

"I'm so hungry now," he said to himself, "I could eat six children before I am full up!"

Just outside the town, there was a pretty little field with trees and bushes all round it. This was called The Picnic Place. There were several wooden tables and long benches, and people were allowed to go there and have a picnic at any time.

The Enormous Crocodile crept over to The Picnic Place. There was no one in sight.

"Now for Clever Trick Number Four!" he whispered to himself.

He picked a lovely bunch of flowers and arranged it on one of the tables.

From the same table, he took away one of the benches and hid it in the bushes.

Then he put himself in the place where the bench had been.

By tucking his head under his chest, and by twisting his tail out of sight, he made himself look very much like a long wooden bench with four legs.

Soon, two boys and two girls came along carrying baskets of food. They were all from one family, and their mother had said they could go out and have a picnic together.

"Which table shall we sit at?" said one.

"Let's take the table with the lovely flowers on it," said another.

The Enormous Crocodile kept
as quiet as a mouse. "I shall eat
them all," he said to himself.
"They will come and sit on
my back and I will swizzle
my head around quickly,
and after that
it'll be *squish
crunch gollop.*"

Suddenly a big deep voice from the jungle shouted, "Stand back, children! Stand back! Stand back!"

The children stopped and stared at the place where the voice was coming from.

Then, with a crashing of branches, Trunky the Elephant came rushing out of the jungle.

"That's not a bench you were going to sit on!" he bellowed. "It's the Enormous Crocodile, and he wants to eat you all up!"

Trunky trotted over to the spot where the Enormous Crocodile was standing, and quick as a flash he wrapped his trunk around the Crocodile's tail and hoisted him up into the air.

"Hey! Let me go!" yelled the Enormous Crocodile, who was now dangling upside down. "Let me go! Let me go!"

"No," Trunky said. "I will not let you go. We've all had quite enough of your clever tricks."

Trunky began to swing the Crocodile round and round in the air. At first he swung him slowly.

Then he swung him faster . . .

And FASTER . . .
And FASTER . . .

And
FASTER
STILL . . .

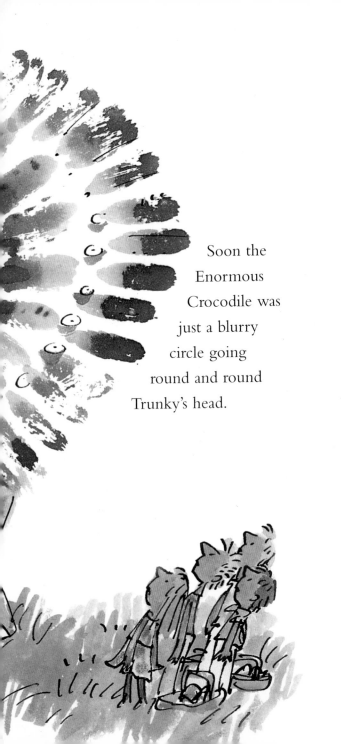

Soon the
Enormous
Crocodile was
just a blurry
circle going
round and round
Trunky's head.

Suddenly, Trunky let go
of the Crocodile's tail,
and the Crocodile went
shooting high up into
the sky like a huge
green rocket.

Up and up he went . . .

HIGHER
and

HIGHER . . .
FASTER
and

FASTER . . .

He was going so fast and so high that soon the earth was just a tiny dot miles below.

He whizzed on and on.

He whizzed far into space.

He whizzed past the moon.

He whizzed past stars and planets.

Until at last . . .

With the most tremendous

BANG!

the Enormous Crocodile crashed
headfirst into the hot hot sun.

And he was sizzled up like a sausage!

THERE'S MORE TO ROALD DAHL THAN GREAT STORIES . . .

Did you know that 10% of author royalties* from this book go to help the work of the Roald Dahl charities?

Roald Dahl is famous for his stories and rhymes, but much less well known is how often he went out of his way to help seriously ill children. Today **Roald Dahl's Marvellous Children's Charity** helps children with the severest conditions and the greatest needs. The charity believes every child can have a more marvellous life, no matter how ill they are, or how short their life may be.

Can you do something marvellous to help others? Find out how at **www.roalddahlcharity.org**

You can find out about Roald Dahl's real-life experiences and how they found their way into his stories at the **Roald Dahl Museum and Story Centre** in Great Missenden, Buckinghamshire (the author's home village). The Museum is a charity that aims to inspire excitement about reading, writing and creativity. There are three fun and fact-packed galleries, with lots to make, do and see (including Roald Dahl's writing hut). Aimed at 6–12-year-olds, the Museum is open to the public and to school groups throughout the year.

Find out more at **www.roalddahlmuseum.org**

Roald Dahl's Marvellous Children's Charity (RDMCC) is a registered charity no. 1137409.
The Roald Dahl Museum and Story Centre (RDMSC) is a registered charity no. 1085853.
The Roald Dahl Charitable Trust is a registered charity no. 1119330 and supports the work of RDMCC and RDMSC.
* Donated royalties are net of commission